To Jack!

PUNK FARM

P.F.

33⅓ RPM   SIDE A

JARRETT J. KROSOCZKA

Dragonfly Books ---✦ New York

The Library of Congress has cataloged the hardcover edition of this work as follows:
Krosoczka, Jarrett.
Punk Farm / Jarrett J. Krosoczka.
p.   cm.
Summary: At the end of the day, while Farmer Joe gets ready for bed, his animals tune their instruments
to perform in a big concert as a rock band called Punk Farm.
ISBN 978-0-375-82429-6 (trade) — ISBN 978-0-375-92429-3 (lib. bdg.)
[1. Musicians—Fiction. 2. Rock music—Fiction. 3. Domestic animals—Fiction. 4. Farm life—Fiction.] I. Title.
PZ7.K935Pu 2005
[E]—dc22
2004018803

ISBN 978-0-440-41793-4 (pbk.)

MANUFACTURED IN CHINA

16 15 14 13 12 11 10
First Dragonfly Books Edition

For my brother,
Richard

Farmer Joe works hard all day long.

At the end of the day, Farmer Joe
is tired and heads home for bed.

Farmer Joe's animals are sleepy, too.
But are they getting ready for bed?

Not tonight.
They have a
show to get
ready for.

Cow sets up
her drums.

Pig plugs in his amp.

Chicken sets up
her keyboards.

Goat tunes his bass.

Sheep checks the microphone. "Testing . . . 1 . . . 2 . . . 3 . . ."

"Okay, gang, tonight's the big night! Let's go over some songs before this place gets packed!"

In the middle of practice, Cow stops drumming.
"Uh . . . guys!" she says. "The farmer's light is on!"

The animals freeze. The microphone screeches.
Footsteps can be heard in the distance.
Will they get caught?

Not tonight. The light goes off, and
Punk Farm finishes their rehearsal.

Outside, animals wait in line and buy tickets.
Everyone is eager for the show to start.

"Are you guys ready?" asks Sheep.
"I was born ready," says Pig.
"Whatever, dude," says Goat.

"I'm nervous," says Chicken.
"Let's do this!" says Cow.

Sheep asks the crowd,
"Who's ready to rock?!"
and they go crazy!

"1-2, 1-2-3-4!"

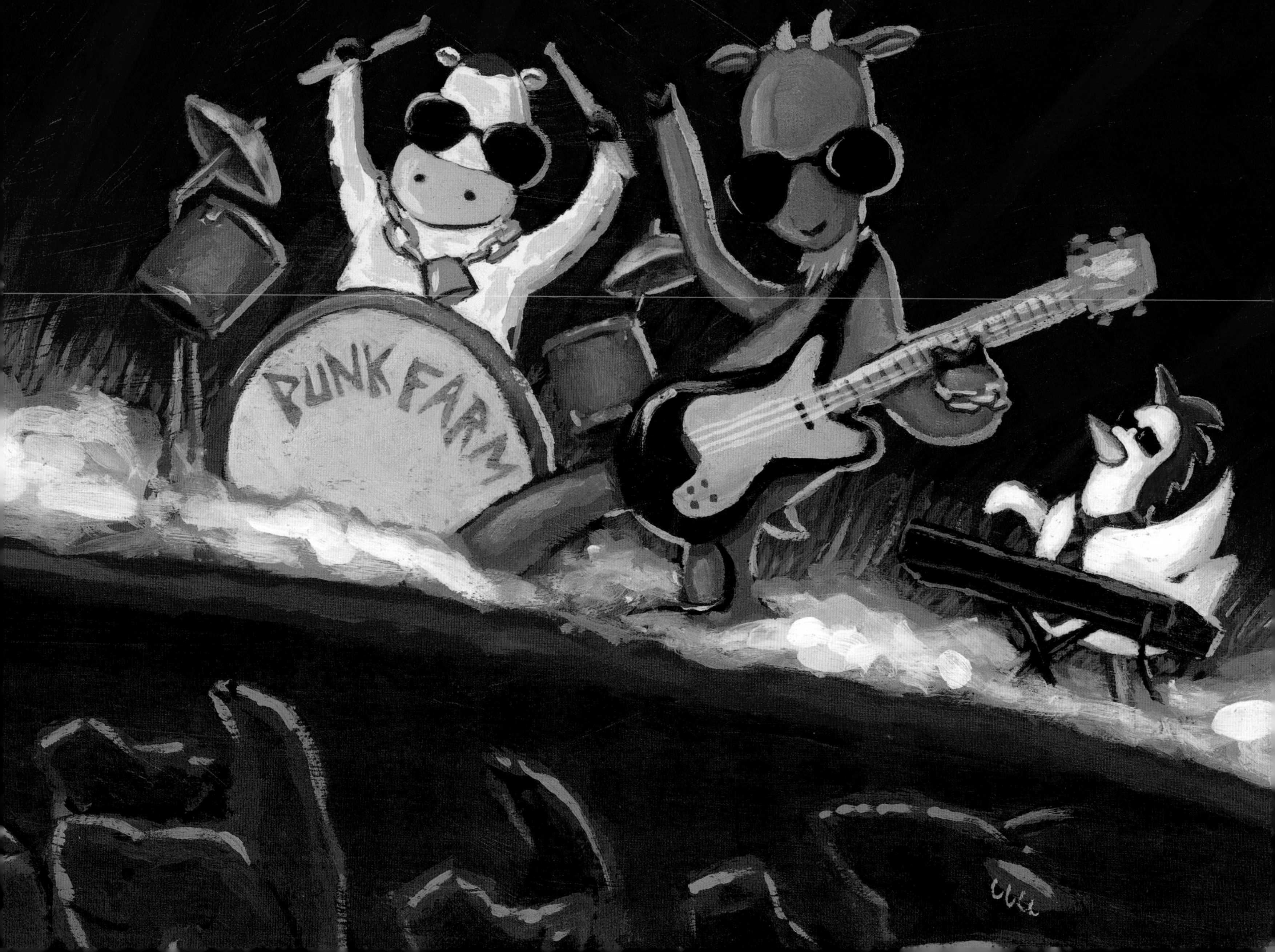

OLD MAC-
DONALD
HAD
A
FARM.

EEE-I-EEE-I-OH!

And on that farm he had a COW!

EEE-I-EEE-I-OH!

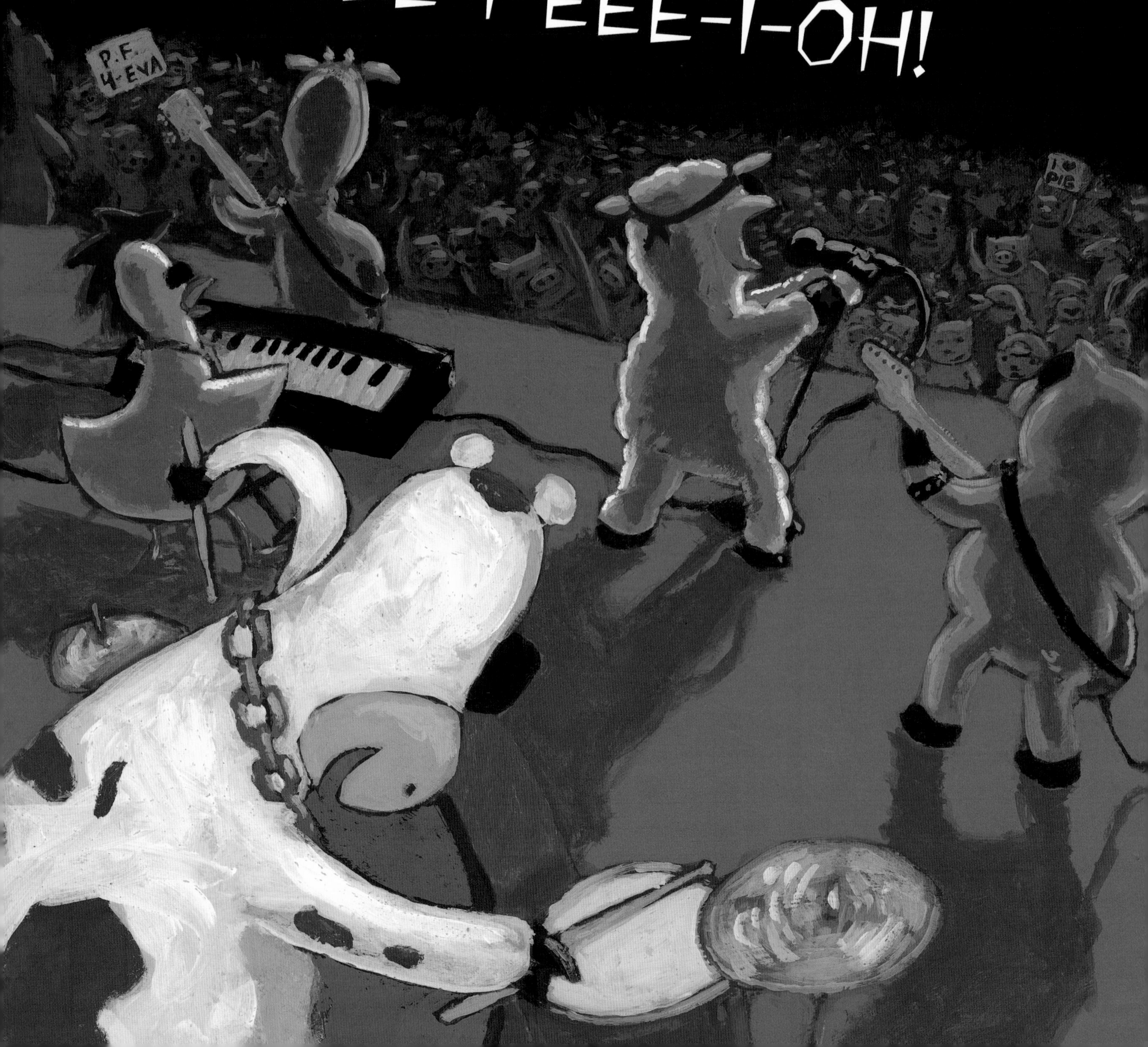

With a BOOM CRASH here
and a BOOM BOOM there.
Here a BOOM, there a CRASH,
everywhere a CRASH
CRASH!

Old MacDonald had a farm!

EEE-I-EEE-I-OH!

And on that farm he had a PIG

EEE-I-EEE-I-OH!

Old MacDonald had a farm!
EEE-I-EEE-I-OH!
And on that farm he had a CHICKEN!
EEE-I-EEE-I-OH!

With a BEEP BEEP here

and a BA BEEP there.

Here a BEEP, there a BEEP,

everywhere a

BEEP

BEEP!

Old MacDonald had a farm!
EEE-I-EEE-I-OH!
And on that farm he had a GOAT!
EEE-I-EEE-I-OH!

With a BRUM BRUM here
and a BA DUM there.
Here a BRUM, there a BRUM,
everywhere a BA DUM!

Punk Farm wails on their instruments one last time and delivers a blazing finale!

EEE-I-EEE-I-

YEEEEEEE

"Thank you, Wisconsin!"

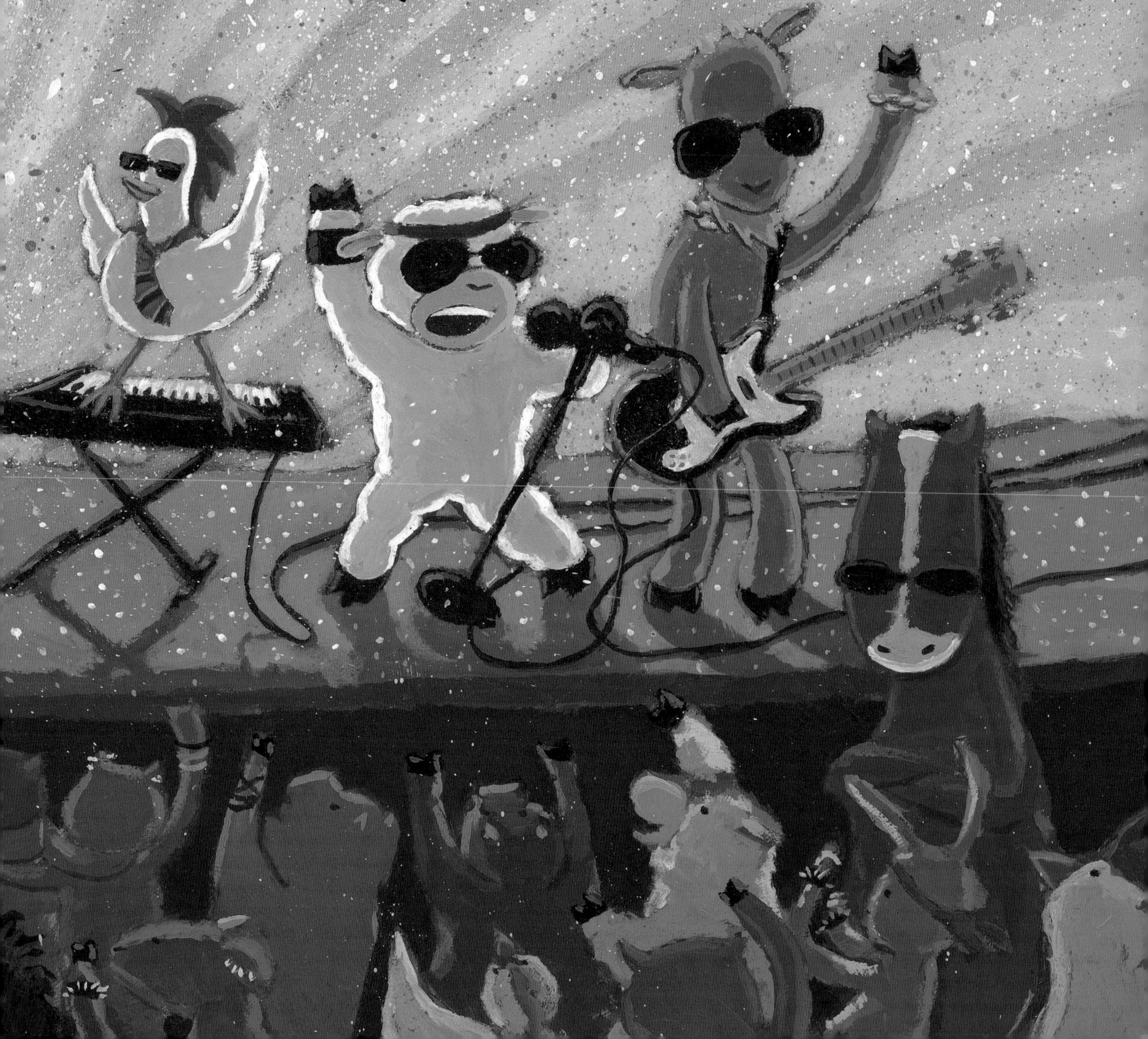

Soon the sun rises and so does Farmer
Joe. He heads over to the barn for . . .

. . . a big day of work.

PUNK FARM IS:

Sheep - vocals

Pig - guitar

Goat - bass

Chicken - keyboards

Cow - drums

We'd like to thank: our families for believing in us. The hole in the wall gang for constantly inspiring us. Green 15 and the London stars! The heroes of the time warp kitchen! All of our friends at Random. everyone down at the barn. And of course—Farmer Joe!

Peace + Rock
Forever,
PUNK FARM

Old MacDonald had a far
EEE-I-EEE-I-OH!
and on that fa
EEE-I-
and